carrying the shadow

carrying the shadow

poems by

Patrick Friesen

*For Shirly,
at West End Cultural Centre,
Oct 16/99
Patrick Frie*

Porcepic Books
an imprint of

Beach Holme Publishing
Vancouver

Copyright © 1999 Patrick Friesen

First Edition

All rights reserved.

No part of this book may be reproduced or transmitted in any form by any means, electronic or mechanical, including photocopying, recording or any information storage, retrieval and transmission systems now known or to be invented, without permission in writing from the publisher, except by a reviewer who may quote brief passages in a review.

This book is published by Beach Holme Publishing, #226—2040 West 12th Ave., Vancouver, BC, V6J 2G2. This is a Porcepic Book.

We acknowledge the financial support of the Canada Council for the Arts, the Government of Canada through the Book Publishing Industry Development Program (BPIDP) and the assistance of the Province of British Columbia through the British Columbia Arts Council for our publishing activities and program.

Editor: Joy Gugeler
Cover Art and Design: Marijke Friesen and Pedro Mendes
Production and Text Design: Teresa Bubela

Canadian Cataloguing in Publication Data

Friesen, Patrick, 1946-
 Carrying the shadow

 Poems.
 ISBN 0-88878-401-5

 I. Title.
PS8561.R496C37 1999   C811'.54   C99-910884-0
PR9199.3.F77C37 1999

In Memory of Roy Vogt

Acknowledgements

Poems from this book appeared in the following: *Canadian Forum, Zygote, Grain, The Capilano Review, Event, Queen Street Quarterly, Rhubarb, and Prairie Fire*. "bled dreams for holy week" appeared in an art exhibit at the Winnipeg Art Gallery. "leaving town" appeared on CBC Radio, "here for its skin" was put to music by Heather McLeod.

"a yellow dress" was put to music by Cate Friesen and appeared on her CD "Joy's Disorder". Cate's website: www.catefriesen.com.

The author would like to thank the Manitoba Arts Council for a major arts grant which helped make this book possible.

Contents

nothing dark	1
shape shifters	2
it goes away	3
lorca's arrows	4
stranger	5
a house shudders	6
rolling home	11
long road	12
here for a minute	13
holding the story	14
the seeding	18
seed	20
christ's arrow	23
bled dreams at holy week	24
almost nothing's written in stone	25
nickname	26
a name has no smell	27
stones lie	29
singing the dead	30
walking the wire	32
god's long pig	35
leaving town	37
first hand	39
waiting	41
visit	42
poem for a dog	44
dark hallway	45
at the foot of the stairs	46
learning braille	47
keeping names	49

obits	*50*
thomas merton and the deer	*51*
richard manuel's grave	*52*
small town	*53*
rural graveyard	*54*
sorrow	*55*
unearthly longing	*56*
fingerprint	*58*
ring around the rosy	*59*
beneath the snow	*60*
poem for a father	*64*
eyelash	*65*
song abandoned	*67*
lamenting these words	*68*
the man who licked stones	*69*
the hidden fire	*70*
gestures of gratitude	*72*
annual physical	*74*
wanting	*76*
fewer questions	*77*
gift	*79*
witness	*80*
arriving	*82*
plum tree	*86*
come with me	*87*
in memorium	*88*
here for its skin	*89*
I will cut you a diamond	*90*
the door	*91*
the hand of my beloved	*92*
empty coat	*94*
dream	*95*
a long footprint	*96*
a yellow dress	*99*
barn's dark door	*100*
caught in the sky	*101*
gravedigger	*102*

home st. 103
joker 104
change change change 105
old tom 106
dead's dead 107
sexton 109
this time around 110
yardwork 111

nothing dark

death is here a river of smiles running through the house
  a red tulip bending in its thirst
a still curtain at noon and a bird fluttering in the eaves the
  screen door slams but no one's there
a hollyhock bleeds on the blinding wall of the house a face
  vanishes from a window
heat rises from the sidewalk the drone of an airplane wandering
  across the sky

reaching for an arrow a child upended in a rain barrel his hands
  scrabbling at the sides
it is only a moment of terror instead of a lifetime of fear there
  are no decisions to be made
someone shot the dog a boy fell from the tree onto barbed wire
  that was one summer
the sun burned a shade into the garden a man on his knees
  that was another

these things these deaths the gorgeous evening and the summer
  night drifting down
there is nothing dark about darkness the sleeping town filled
  with shadows
a willow near the well and a silver birch a cat straying through
  the night
the call you hear laughter from a doorway and air stirring
  in the leaves

shape shifters

children on their backs
clouds shifting above them
whispering old stories

sitting on a stone
singing a lullaby
only the dead hear

the distant hooves
of startled horses
on their way to the horizon

it goes away

a garden behind a house
smelling the mint
a bench in a clearing
feeling the sun

it goes away

a long-legged daughter on the grass
watching her dance
a son swaying in the willow
listening to him laugh

it goes away

a hand tracing your face
tasting its salt
a body asleep beside you
feeling her breath

it goes away

a black dog at your door
smelling its heat
a white horse in your dream
listening to the hooves

it goes away

lorca's arrows

lorca's arrows
without targets
san sebastian's arrows
without end

the ecstasy of arrows
arcing across the field
a child's dreams
forever in mid-flight

growing out of summer
into dark clothes
holding hands
where the river flows

stranger

a black shirt and no tie
a man in his suit
is staring at his shoes
the dust on them
and on the blades of grass

the narrow asphalt road
shimmers with heat
and the remembered sound
of tires sucking on tar

his hands in his jacket pockets
he looks up at the name
his fingers play with a button
and the ashes along a seam

a woman's voice drifts
across the lawns
calling her children
there's a stranger
in the graveyard

a house shudders

a house shudders
struck by a comet
windows burst
and a door hangs
on one hinge

on another street
a house stands unchanged
though the lights go out
and a stillness echoes
like water around a stone

tell the lilac about your house
when the curtain parts
and the air shifts
tell the willow
when grief arrives

{What we used to call 'not all there', kind of an interesting phrase if you think on it. I mean I know I'm not always all there, you get what I mean? Off in some other land, preoccupied, dreaming.

Nevertheless, what you could see of him was very much on the fence in front of the post office all afternoon. Sitting there, spitting seeds. It got disgusting sometimes, after he'd been there four or five hours and gone through a few large bags. You'd see people doing a little jog to avoid the pile of seeds, wet with spittle and just not very appetizing.

I joked to him once that he'd better watch his heart what with all the salt he was taking in with the seeds. Next time he caught sight of me-I was actually on the other side of the street-he called out my name real loud. I couldn't for the life of me tell where the voice was coming from.

When I finally looked across the street, there he was on the fence clutching at his chest. His mouth opened, and he fell on his back to the ground. By the time I got across the street, he was surrounded by people. I saw one eye peep open, and he started laughing. Sat up, shook out a handful of seeds, and offered them.

Thinking of him lying on his back like that reminds me of an attack I saw when I was young. The stonelicker. He's over there somewhere, in the older section. Let me show you.

I just knew him as the stonelicker because he walked around town, sticking to the gravel roads, always wearing a dirty, long coat, didn't matter how hot it was. It must have been for the deep pockets. He'd stop, pick up a stone, hold it up, turning it to get good light on it, and lick it, look again, then put it in a pocket or drop it. Didn't know why he licked them until my mother said it was to get the dust off, so he could see the grain in the stone, or the colors.

I think there was more to it than that. We have five senses. Sometimes I think we've got another one or two. I figure the stonelicker was getting to know something about those stones. The taste, maybe, but the feel of it too, the feel he couldn't get with his fingers. The tongue is more delicate, explores in its own way, finds the splits and folds the fingers pass over.

Ah...

A suicide. See, stone's facing west, away from the resurrection. Didn't know him that well, not many did. Turned out his own family didn't really know him. There are stories, but...well, he made sure there was an end to him. Set his barn on fire, then hung himself from a rafter.

Stonelicker was a thin man, and that long coat made him look even thinner. Grey hair, never combed, unshaven. A pale man, but very red lips. You noticed them, a red mouth and the rest of him kind of bloodless.

He should be right here.

No, that's not him. Must be a row over.

Strange, that's not him either.

All of a sudden I don't know where he is, don't know where I am. All these stones, you can lose your way.

Anyway, stonelicker. My friend and I were walking along the street, it was winter, probably January or February. I noticed stonelicker up ahead on the street crossing ours. He got over the intersection when, just like that, he stops, his feet still moving, but he's going in a circle, turning around, maybe three times, his feet kicking out like he's walking.

He stops, stands there straight as a rod, then falls on his back. It was something to see. When a person falls he protects himself, puts his hands out, or bends so he doesn't hit the ground full force, but stonelicker falls back tall and straight, arms at his sides, bang on his back.

We ran over. Stonelicker's eyes are wide open, he's breathing hard, snot coming out of his nose, his mouth foaming, his legs trembling.

Those eyes didn't see us, just staring at the sky, fixed like that. Blue and glazed over, like wet stones.

It was something.

He sure fell in the right place-in front of the pastor's house, and across the street and a few doors down from the undertaker's.

Read in the newspaper that he died in the hospital.}

rolling home

dark tires roll
in the afternoon sun
past the lumber yard
its fragrant white planks
past the post office
red brick and flag
the old schoolhouse
with its sepia windows
and children on the swings
past the hardware store
all hammer hinge and glue
rolling along the black asphalt
and its tendril waves of heat
the tires rolling
with the smell of rubber
the dark casket
ominous inside
the chrome and tinted glass
of the hearse
rolling through the intersection
past the pharmacist in his doorway
an old man and his dog
past the bicycle leaning
against a wall
rolling toward the edge of town
bone-white stones
and poplar leaves fluttering
silver in the breeze
rolling home
rolling home

long road

it bends through the graveyard long road taken snaking
through the long day
slow wheels in the dust and mirage the sun glinting off chrome
and black paint
feels like forever in the heat the smell of mown grass and damp
clay beside the grave
feels like forever six young men in their suits their eyes down
carrying the shadow before them

we work tirelessly toward that day turning the earth with our
ploughs and scouring the sky
each of us all tooth and nail and brain inventing death with our
hunger again and again
who's got the time to stop who's keeping time do we get to
wind our watches?
who's the undertaker in town who's the sexton do we get to
know them in the end?

we're looking for someone at the station when the train pulls in
someone meant for us
arms full of roses in love in love ashes to ashes in the name of
in the name of in the name

here for a minute

I was here for a minute
buried my father in may
my grandparents in winter
buried schoolmates
slaughtered in cars
or down by fire
I was here
just passing through
on this winding road
the black hearse parked there
the sun sparkling in its mirror
I carried them to their graves
wearing a dark jacket and tie
and sunday shoes
I was here for a moment
full-throated and mourning
what I didn't know
I was here
alive and deaf
as stones
my shadow beside the hole
and blackbirds whistling

holding the story

who will hold the story
of the boy gone bad
looking for god behind God
looking for the particulars
the poplar tree on the corner of the lot
the garden's deep dream

who will hold the story
when the man's memory falters
looking for his shoes
looking through the cellar
yellow packets of letters
and anecdotes in the attic

who will hold the story
of the last day
looking through the mirror
looking through the dark
the nightstand with its lamp
and a glass of water

{Never knew anyone baked a better apple pie. Green apples. Just tart enough but sweet. Won prizes at the fair more than twice. All her cooking was tops, or so I've heard. Never tasted anything besides the pie myself. And it's been a while since I've been able to eat green apples.

Kept a fantastic garden. People would go by for walks on Sundays just to stare at that garden. The vegetables as pretty as the flowers, the way she laid everything out. You'd see her out there for hours every day come summer.

But what I give her most credit for is how she raised those kids, and she had a few. Every one of them grew up right. Decent and civil and gumption at the same time. Stood up for themselves, they did, but seldom a vile word about anyone.

All of them in good jobs. You know what I mean? Work that they love, that serves humanity. Carrying their share, and more. I give the credit to their mother.

Dead by thirty-five. But you lay the groundwork early and everything's possible.

Walking down her street on a summer's night, piano music floating through the soft air in June. Even if she was teaching, and you could hear her play the scales, even that sounded wonderful.

Not like the violin. Worse than cats in heat because at least you know the cats have to do what they're doing, and there'll be more cats down the line. But the piano always sounds so clear.

Well I always made sure I went for my evening walk about 8:30, the last lesson over, and she playing for her own pleasure.

She knew I went for my walk then. She told me once, we were both buying vegetables in the grocery, she told me she appreciated my shadow outside her window. Said it was nice to play for an audience.

She played all of them. Beethoven, Mozart, Bach. But I always liked Schubert best. Especially, his lieder. She had a voice, too, that one. Like a bird.

Hearing that soprano drifting down the street, through the leaves, I imagine that's what heaven sounds like. And I guess it does now that she's there.

Named one of my boys after something she played. A piece of music that could make you cry, something real slow. It must have been a favorite because she played it a lot.

That time I ran into her in the grocery I asked her about it. She said it was an "adagio". So, my second son has that for his middle name. Adagio. Mind you, he hates it. Doesn't ever let on that he has it. One day, I figure, he'll hear that piece of music, and I mean really hear it, and he'll feel blessed.

The poultryman had a great laugh. Rising from his belly and raucous through his throat. A straw hat and a long-sleeved shirt always buttoned at the wrists and at the neck. Over this shirt, coveralls. He said he wore the long-sleeved shirt, and long underwear beneath that, to keep cool in the summer.

"Like the Bedouin," he'd laugh.

The legs of his coveralls always seemed to be misted with a dark spray. Like it was paint.

Many times I saw his hatchet come down. I was fascinated by that moment. He pinned the wings back holding the chicken firmly with one powerful paw. Lowered to the block, a tree stump, the chicken blinking. The hatchet crunched its neck, the body in convulsions, blood spurting.

They used to kill kings and queens that way.

One day I was standing nearby, watching him catch a chicken for the stump. This time, when the blade severed the head, he let go the chicken. Its head staring, lying on the ground beside the stump, the body ran circles around the poultry man, blood pumping into the air, and the poultryman, watching my horror, my open mouth, roared with laughter.

When I walked over to look more closely, I couldn't find any blood, only a dampness drying in the soil.}

the seeding

this is where it begins
the words they call memory
a moment a turn
human motion shifting
to story
shaping and timing
talking toward completion

it begins in this garden
the seeding
the body broken
from the world
and buried
in the earth
it begins
when rain comes
slanting home

and I could tell you
a story so true
and sorrowful
I could tell you
the days of life
each breath
a gesture of the hand
I could tell you
the hour
how it happened
once
and never again

I bury the dead
and grieve them
and slowly

learn the stories
they earned
a blackbird singing
on a fencepost

seed

the seed here
grows words
weather chisels the stone
grass soil and flesh
these layers
nothing remembered
in the end
nothing but the stones
engraved
graven images
and the endless worship
of the dead

fearing
not death
but the end
of memory
the story
dismembered
again and again
the necessary fictions
saying 'I was'
'I will be'
but unable to say
'I am'

that hidden moment
coming with child
the first seam sewn
the molecule quickened
like the coming together
of fire and air
all that undone
here finally

in this field
where flesh and spirit split
the weld
gives way
world sundered
from word

{Just like it happened yesterday, it's that clear. The sun going down slowly and the air so still. I remember a hammer in the distance. Echoing. It was twilight, with that hush, and the hammer, and his head turning toward me, he said "building my house". And him just a day away from heaven.}

christ's arrow

christ's arrow
and the ecstatic body
shuddering
its last orgasm

a holy day
eyes gawking
and a gaping mouth
filled with earth

ask the lilac
where beauty is
ask the willow
for its tears

bled dreams at holy week

blood cloistered
with the thick smell
of incense and wax

the dust and dull gold
of petrified flesh
air dense with gangrene

the mortified body
coiling and uncoiling
and shucking its skin

flayed and raw
and raised
above the human parade

almost nothing's written in stone

only what's kept
names dates and epigraphs
the banalities of death

nothing gets written in stone

not what matters
the fish stories and fibs
flimflams and howlers
all the woven yarns

nothing in stone
no human hand
nothing but earth's slow fire
cooling
and the relentless weather

nickname

after all the names
surname and christian
after initials and dates
when born married or dead
after fine words
and longing
there is nothing left
but history
nothing breathes

but there is a headstone
with something more
a name that claims
a moment absolutely
caught between two names
water it reads
and I don't know
why or what
but it's there
a significance a man apart
named beside a stream
the sea or a ditch
a boy with a soaker
or upended in a rain barrel
a young man
swimming through time

a name has no smell

overrun by pigs and weeds
stones toppled in the grass
beneath july heat
this unkempt graveyard
is the record

my long-ago grandmother
someone tall and blonde
from photographs
her strong hands holding an apple
her smile squinting into the sun
behind the camera

it astonishes me
that her hands look like mine
it's not something I knew
the woman long dead
in those early winter months
as the war was ending
a young woman shaking off
earth's labour
and gone to ground
here

a pig rooting among the thistles
near her stone
chickens pecking and clucking
in the stillness
the war over the flu done
history stopped dead here
her white body
lowered here with her voice
and memory
chiselled into granite

a name
for a grandson to remember
a name for a body
he never saw or heard
a body he never touched
a name grows older
than memories
a name has no smell

its snout in damp earth
the pig grunts
a hawk swooping low
over a stubble field
already I remember
and the world dies
a little more

stones lie

the stones lie
no one came from this town
no one died on this date
no one born
the stones lie
there was no one
by that name

white stones
scattered in grass
like newspapers in the wind
their dark headlines
and the lies
between the lines
they hold

and the one
without a name or stone
the one who asked
only to live
in our hearts
the one who vanished
into everything
is laughing
and laughing

singing the dead

singing the dead
their tongues stilled
singing what falls
in the grass
the sparrow no one sees
a pebble from a shoe
a footprint
singing what grass teaches
our numbered days
the years that crumble
into the lies
of time
eternity stretching out
before and after
each date on these stones
each stone here
on this ground
the astonishing centre
of forever

{My first corpse, the first one I saw, was probably about 1930 when I was four or five years old. I was at funeral with my parents. There was a long sermon. I wasn't listening. My eyes were fixed on that black casket at the front of the church. I knew there was someone inside it. It was so black. After a while people got up from their pews and began filing past the open casket. I remember a lot of crying, the air thick with something. Like before a prairie storm. I could taste the air. She was a woman at least 80 years old, in a black dress and a black shawl on her head. But what I remember most, though, and it's stayed with me ever since, was a large iridescent blowfly sitting on her dead mottled cheek. I wanted to vomit, felt myself gagging. But the fly, shimmering green and blue, the fly was beautiful.}

walking the wire

everything begins and ends
with a cliche
we are what we are
nothing more
an accumulation of days
births and deaths
running back
as far as you can imagine
and more

family heat and betrayals
sheet lightning across the sky
the heavy hand
and the martyr's sigh
all the human instruments
of negotiation
loneliness and fear
slow words across the back fence
sermons the cold eye some love is
sorrow and hidden rage
submission with its ecstasy and cost
all the beliefs of pain
man and woman entwined
spitting like ancient snakes
caressing their bodies
teeth at each other's throats
in love

but who judges?
who has the heart?
who can read the heart?
read it and read
until your eyes burn out
then read it blind

with your fingers
read it when it gives you joy
when it lacerates
read the human heart
your heart
is old old old
reptilian and feathered
a stone a burning tulip
a pouch of blood
read the other heart
the invented heart
which holds a love
that brings the world alive
for a moment
lancelot and guinivere
love that doesn't know
the calendar
or the second hand
sweeping round and round
holy mother
love that doesn't know
its own good

the sun blazing
you can almost hear its inferno
as it boils across the sky
year after year
the cries of love
and horror
the endless deaths
the unbearable pleasures
of tooth and hand

I have words
I speak and write
I light a match
in the mirror

someone there
has written
my names
one for the right hand
one for the other
my names are my tribes
I live between them
arms outstretched
and walking the wire

god's long pig

you want dignity
human flair
beauty and the saint
I confess
to yearning for the flesh
a little elegance
a fine ankle
and a narrow foot
fashion and red nails
on my knees
at the stations
looking for an end
some smoke
to show the way

a corpse
fat and farting
beneath the sun
a bloated mess
of cells
unstrung
and unsung
home
for the blowfly
earth's feast
the flowering
entrails
the famished mouth
open for a kiss
who will kiss
this man?

carrion
waits for god
how else
redemption?
and the desert
funnels in
at its ears
and mouth
the meat
drifting away
on the sand
god's
long pig
going to bone
and something
less

your bulova
with its rubies
and diamond precision
your cuff links
your tie pin
you are out of style
your jeans
and your sandals
your 5 o'clock
shadow
you too are out of style
with your jazz
and your cigarillos
there is room
for you
in heaven

leaving town

the room is empty but the door's still swinging on its hinge
  who's been there?
someone's missing you can see where he stood in the photo
  the full absent length of him
hands on hips long and lean all bones inside his suit he turns
  squinting into the sun

someone's son who stumbled into the mirror saw at last
  what had always been there raw nerve and wires
he found his road long legs raising dust
his thumb out hitching his way toward god
the way god sometimes whispers over a shoulder with the
  unbearable fineness of a fallen hair
and sometimes rushes across the open field an unknowable
  wind and storm

who's the long man walking through town?

the town's so small and so much going on behind doors
all the whispers and secrets who's creeping in the back way?
who's hiding bottles behind the wall?
there's gossip at the cafe and the sun passing toward noon
fingers at the curtains in the window

who is the man who walked through town?
he never did belong whose son is he?

a child's desire to be held
the hired hand whacking the head off a hen
blood sprouting like scarlet stars against the sky
he takes everything in where does it go?
there's so much light in the world it's hard to see
the abandoned boy becoming man

there's no home for anger
and his shoes have worn out

thunder's rolling in prairie's rolling in horizon rolling in
he's kneeling into the train everyone's got a train to meet
he's silent as he waits his pockets stuffed with words
kneeling in his surrender on a prairie line
the smell of clover and dust
the squeal of wheels on the tracks

who's the man who left town?
the man who lost all his words
who had electricity in his veins
he stepped out of the photograph into light
and they're still talking in the cafe

first hand

I've seen death
first hand
someone beloved
passing
from light breath
and pain
to something else
something grey
beneath his skin
something hardening
his eyes
I've seen death once
at first hand
and it's all I needed
to know the approaching night
would be the first ever
the sun in may
lowering through the birch
the evening's stillness
arriving like a veil
some invisible bird
twittering outside the window
just for a moment
like a soul
singing in the branches
of a tree
and I knew the morning
would come too
and I would breathe
more deeply
smell the first lilacs
sharply

the world entering once again
and taking me
over
yellow light
through venetian blinds
the sticky ring
a water glass left
on the bedside table
the silt of a last sleep
in the corners of his eyes
nothing to say
but the words
struggling to be true

waiting

think of them
thousands
lying here
sleeplessly
beneath your feet
in their suits
and dresses
waiting and
waiting

visit

a light
in the window
to show the way
an empty dish
to welcome you back

memory
is the door
left ajar

the way you cleared your throat
before you spoke
but never found the words
waving the moment away
with your beautiful hand

the lord
was in your eyes
one blind
the other dying

it's been a while
since we've talked
you never say anything
in the graveyard
and you haven't come around

I no longer
have much to say
I find the words
but they're worn

as if I ground down your bones
and swallowed

I am your grave
and carry you around

let's visit
in silence
kiss my mouth
and bless me
I'll hold you
and give you
my heart

my child
my son
my father

the door's open
there's light
for your feet
I'm ready
for you
at last

poem for a dog

yearning like a child for the sky's pale blue distance what I knew
 then and am coming to again the night of forever lit by the sun
 lying on my back in tall grass staring until sightless at the
 impossibility of it all nothing to untangle only wonder and a
 simple faith in light

world that the old ones hated or pretended to hate their
 unbearable rebellion against leaf and flesh their fear of
 themselves
god in everything in darkness and light each thing lit from inside
 because it is because it is a small sun each thing for a moment
 blessing the world

I stood beside the back door in 1956 looking at the camera my
 mother held today I look at the photo me staring (at myself and
 back again)
if there hadn't been a camera I would still be gazing back and
 forth through the lies of memory and imagination I would
 still be lost in light

oreo pads silently into this room and lies beside my chair our
 eyes meet like they did before when I was a boy and he had
 another name
he fears the thunder rolling in from the mountains it sounds like
 guns trust has been broken and will be again we live with
 broken words

I haven't forgotten the dog how he lit the afternoon one summer
 I haven't forgotten the boy living in light I carry him truer than
 photographs
and oreo grows old at my feet a black dog from nowhere rain
 pelting down on the skylight and voices from long ago
 everywhere

dark hallway

from this chair
in the bright room
I hear the dog's nails
clicking down the hallway
the door open a crack
to darkness
and I think I see
this black dog
perhaps his eyes
looking at me
then I'm not sure
and the longer I stare
the less I see
until at last it seems
a movement
of black on black
the dog passing by

when I open the door
there's nothing
and I call out *boy*
forgetting that's not his name
but the name of my youth
another dog
another time
I look both ways
down the dark hallway
so familiar so strange
the sigh of a breath
and the stars in my eyes
flicker from far
as I turn
in the doorway

at the foot of the stairs

the dog asleep
at the foot of the stairs

the cat watching
from the top step

so far to travel
in this house

elegant shoes
beside the door

a black vase
filled with leaves

mulling my way
toward heaven

learning braille

learning braille
to find what's hidden
in the granite letters
blind with recollections
the family photos
abandoned clothes
hanging in their closets
blind with a thousand details

the way the late sun
lit the wall of a house
a golden window
turning black
as a summer storm
closed in

the way a curtain
shivered
as the wind woke
then parted
to reveal a face

just that moment
those staring eyes
hands on the sill
and a few plump drops
of rain

a moment
where she's not a mother
nor daughter
a moment
where she's hardly human
someone lost

at the edge of the house
and looking at the sky

the smell
of the approaching rain
and the air electric
around her impassive face
it's in my hands
my fingers delving
into hidden places
feeling the loneliness
and the secrets there
it's in my hands
the stone's relief
how light fingers
the words

keeping names

keeping names
a man
his feet in europe
his heart in the wind
intentions
best or mediocre
the heart saying 'speak
the wheel is turning'

mother lullabies
the baby in its cradle
singing her children
toward death
peter and mary
and henry and ann

keeping names
something human that remains
a museum for memory
keeping names
until they've bled their story
the facts collapse
and we all fall down
husha husha

obits

here's a kind face
our lenience
merciful words
and bearable
man woman and child
something written and said
the bare facts
something remembered
a story growing

we miss them all
and they tug at us
with a thread
we wipe our eyes
and tug back
the umbilical
never goes slack

thomas merton and the deer

thomas merton
and the deer
their fear
and tender eyes
as they watched him
at dawn
moving through
his stations
his mountain
how he scaled it
or almost
dying near the top
was he climbing
or rappelling
his way down?
on the doorstep
you might say
leaving or entering
a monk
in bare feet
and silent
lurching
to the floor
past kneeling
prostrate
in a pool of water
and perhaps
remembering
for a moment
the deer
in kentucky
at the edge
of the clearing

richard manuel's grave

felt like a brother
there
in march
a thin coat
shivering
in the snow
a brother
and the song
dead
in his throat

small town

a dog sleeps in the sunlight
someone's playing harmonica
I'm waiting for something to happen

a '56 chevy rounds the corner
the banker singing a hymn
his arm signaling the turn

four crows on the roof
I'm thinking of a carpenter
hauling shingles up the ladder

the mid-afternoon is silent
and still as a photograph
in the unearthly heat

everything's a secret
grandmother in the garden
her apron stained with raspberries

a cat stretches on the top step
then slowly descends
into the world

a bicyclist blowing
through the shrubs
his legs thrown wide

bells are ringing
it's another wedding
bride and groom at the door

rural graveyard

blackbird
on a fencepost
scrawny wild rose
in the barbed wire

and the sun boils down

a farmer
ploughing his field
gulls floundering
over the furrows

and the sun boils down

a minister
in his dark suit
paging through
the black book

and the sun boils down

sorrow

there is sorrow in the song a voice as rough as dirt sung from a
  ragged throat
there is pain in the longing no answers and nothing to answer for
  there is so little

love grows like a sadness the dead know this they sing of nothing
  else but love
they sing of lost love the lover never found they sing of love that
  is always out of reach

each has journeyed through time there is no other way there is no
  salvation in knowledge
in the end they have all acknowledged their footsteps in kitchens
  and halls on narrow paths

one was halfway up a ladder another on her knees in the garden
  a third lay asleep
they all walked to the clearing walking through the world the
  body of god in all its weathers

there is a sorrow greater than death a sorrow that runs through
  ecstasy toward surrender
the heart's sorrow rooted there in clay longing for earth a hand
  on a foot

unearthly longing

singing to me
his mouth filled with dirt
with dark words
and underground rhythms
singing implacably
full-throated
possessed by death's charisma

death's song
is a yellow light
on a wicker chair
beneath a shaded lamp
it is a song of eternity
the unearthly longing
for someone
who can never be

it sings a pain
that lives behind
a hand waving
or a smile
it sings behind everything
slowly beautifully
a haunting
of the heart

a rough voice
not easily broken
always breaking
at dawn
the pain of waking
again and again
and waiting
the restless song

seeping through earth
all woven
and dark timbre
and rising
like a shadow
at noon

fingerprint

this is not death
these names
these crates of bones

the town goes to work
the dead walking
the streets at noon

the music teacher
listens to the wind
with perfect pitch

we are parts
of the weather
light sifting through

this is not death
these ashes
this sinking stone

the fingerprint
at the window
there's death

when it's still
you can hear it
scratching at the door

ring around the rosy

children on the grass
miles from nowhere
no entrances or exits
forever
children
beneath the sun

winding among the stones
playing *ring around the rosy*
dancing above the bones
their *pockets full of posey*

voices in the air
their words harmless
as they play at death
leapfrogging stones
or wading
through their reflections

winding among the stones
playing *ring around the rosy*
dancing above the bones
their *pockets full of posey*

in the beginning
their mouths gaping
for a breath
at noon
four and twenty blackbirds
in the heat

all fall down

beneath the snow

snow falls silently
across the graveyard
drifting into the evergreens
onto the headstones
and nestling softly
in the names and numbers
until they're gone

could be any town
lights fading in the flurry
joyce's dublin
prague or steinbach
could be any history
if we had ears to hear
ancient horses galloping
through the snow
or drums in the forest

the blasted world
is the sacrament
each day's work and disease
this is what we know
thefts and grace
the howling heart
our bodies going down
what we adore and kiss
disappearing
beneath the snow

{Wife and mother.

You wouldn't put that on a headstone today, I don't think. And look here, her husband, same thing.

Husband and father.

Wife or husband, father, mother. What else was there? Nothing but your soul, and that was between you and the Lord.

Your soul, your soul.

The car dealer, here, he wanted something more. Brought the first car into these parts. Must have been around 1920. Drove it in with its racket and dust. Church leaders told him he'd go to hell for bringing the devil's contraption in. He didn't scare that easily. Started selling cars, slowly at first, then everyone had to have one.

Interesting, how the more you have, the more you need. Ever notice that? Once you start building, there's no end to it. You have to keep building, repairing, and what not.

When I stop to smell the air, see all the blacktop where there used to be fields, I wonder if maybe those ministers weren't right. For the wrong reasons.

But, never mind me, I like to tell stories. My daughter says the only way they'll know I'm dead is when I stop talking. As if that will stop me.

I'd forgotten his name. Just knew him as Nails. Everyone called him that. You'd walk past a house he was working on, call out a greeting, and he'd just turn and nod his head, his mouth bristling with nails. The hammer still moving through thin air, him reaching for one of those nails, and then turning back to work.

Always building, even at home in the evening. Some addition or other. Never got around to repairing anything because nothing had the time to go into disrepair. Hammer and nails and saw.

And measuring things. I can still see him standing in front of his doorway, a pencil stuck between his cap and ear, measuring the door with his careful eye. Then reaching into his apron for that fat tape measure of his. Measuring. Everything got measured. He must have known the dimensions of the whole town.

He even talked like that. Everything had its length, or was a particular distance from something else. He'd hold his hands out, apart. "To St. Pierre? 12 and 1/8 miles if the wind's at your back." Funny man.

No children. Quiet kind of wife. Heard they'd eloped. Must have been in their early twenties. She never left the house. You'd see her passing by the windows. Mind you, Sundays, she'd be in the back pew with Nails. I never really talked with her. And Nails without any nails in his mouth. You'd say hello, nice day, and he'd nod. I guess when you get into a way of doing things, you pretty well stick to it.

Nice man. Nodding his head and all those nails in his mouth. Killed him too. Those nails. Died of lead poisoning twenty, twenty-one, years ago.}

poem for a father

I return your wallet and your scar
I would gladly exchange them for a face
something to confront each day's confusion

I've been watching the boy
some days he grows tough
other days he's knocked out in the heat

I've watched him on the beach
digging among the rocks
stopping to stare across the water

he doesn't know what he's looking for
it's a code in his bones
that drives him toward memory

he gave me your wallet
having spent all he needed
and wanting some other name

eyelash

the sun rises each morning
but all that's left of him
is an eyelash
caught in the dust
of his glasses
and his pocket watch
on the dresser

who knows
when grief begins
or when it ends?
you may as well
tell time
its work
you may as well
close memory
in your fist

one day you notice
the eyelash is gone
and the dust thicker
on the lens
one day you see
the watch has run
pooling on the dresser
and leaking
off the edge

one morning you wake
on a beach
and you lie there
in the sand
beneath the sun
staring at the watch

who knows
where the eyelash is?
a breeze
through the window
and somewhere
a solar wind

song abandoned

your fingerprints on the telephone the way you raised your
  chin when you coughed
your slow humour sliding through conversations showing your
  teeth when you laughed
your mystery the boy flying away just like that all goodbyes
  and see you in heaven
your sorrow I imagined I didn't think I'd see you again that this
  life was enough

my father is spread all over the sky his long narrow feet his
  forearms and his eyes
my father has vanished nothing familiar left behind nothing but
  an old suit
my father is not my father is not father at all my father is
  becoming something else
my father is the tree he was as he fell he is the axe and the
  muscle my father is the air I breathe

we grieve what we lose the smell of him his hands his voice
  singing hymns him at the door
we grieve what we remember the earthly man what we gather
  from scraps of smoke
we grieve what haunts us the man torn from the photo the
  astonishing absence
we grieve what becomes us the last secret the badly-kept secret
  the ashes of our names

I let fall a son's duty let fall what was promised in my name
  I let fall the name
I assert myself for a little while a thin candle or a single cell
  from the sea a man
I am watery flowing away more quickly than I think a river I
  have dreamed before
I say I on earth and say my piece tatters of cloth and air the
  song abandoned

lamenting these words

lamenting these words how they came to be how that moment
  arrived when I spoke and father dropped me
in fear lamenting the colors and striations the fume and smoke
  of words how I broke into their beauty and lost myself
these words drifting between us clouds of spoken breath veiling
  our eyes our hands at our sides
these words shifting inside the heart and muscle slipping into
  the blood the world fading at noon

rilke knowing this from his castle from the eagle's air almost
  knowing wordlessness
words like notes getting in the way of the song the feel what the
  hand knows and the tongue
I want to talk without words or pluck them hammering them
  until the heart knows
the world rolling in my arms my feet shucking their shoes and
  stepping into the kicking horse river

a baptism old man losing myself like you disappeared from the
  road's shoulder
how you gave yourself over in the fall's heat the wheat pale and
  the lord in your heart
I know the cost of words where they took me I know your pain
  when you let me go
I want to tell you I'm working for the world you left I want to tell
  you I'm still working for you

the man who licked stones

the man in the long coat licked stones memorizing the world's
   first fire on his tongue
he didn't have time to speak though he had nothing else he
   hadn't come to words
his slow hands hung from the stillness of his torn sleeves
   reaching only to touch what he might remember
with his hands he carefully brushed dust from stones with his
   tongue revealed their rose or cobalt blue
he walked outside town on gravel roads he walked outside love
   too close to worship to say
around him earth's rubble and striations sign and witness of the
   forge he longed to find
his mouth craving volcanoes the taste of ash and rain his mouth
   ground stones in his sleep
I thought he would vanish one day spellbound in his cellar
   among the coal and roots
I thought in the end he might walk into the river with his heavy
   pockets but there was no such privilege for him
with the years I forgot him or he became a shape I couldn't see
   wandering around town
I don't know if he took form again or if it was time for me to see
   but I saw him emerge like a photograph in its bath
he was walking past the church he reeled suddenly with a
   stiff-legged pivot and fell straight on his back
no one falls like that the body in surrender to gravity no one falls
   as if nothing matters and nothing did
his eyes glistening like wet sapphires in snow his dead eyes
   looked through us seeing their way into stone

the hidden fire

where was the fire hidden?

spinning, now, here
where he stood
in this room
a wheel of flame
unfleshed, the terrifying soul
passing by a last time
a farewell to this place
no longer son brother or father
serrated, a buzz saw of fire
before man
shaped a civilization
of himself
and after all
fell down

where was the fire?

this man in his galoshes
walking to work
the deepest sorrow
in his heart
this man lit with love
on earth
not the cold fire
of old stars

the impersonal sea
in his loins
the comedy of sex
in all its gravity
the man with scriptures
on his knees

where was the fire?

hunger and laughter
his working hands
the man burned away leaving nothing
but fire
itself

whirling here in the dead of night
his body buried
this fire
revealing itself
unafraid undressed and unattached

I grieve less
the self stops calling into the void
a nostalgia
for a patch of flesh
and person

fire scares
my walls falling away
this is death
a return
to old light

a man
taking leave
without a gesture
vanishing
from the child

the fire
though
the fire
is
in me

gestures of gratitude

the wind twists on the beach turns whirling and passes through
   us my hat flying away
we hold on to each other almost blown into the sea lovers
   hanging on beneath the sun
you stare after the twister crossing water your back to me as if
   you are going away
I know you're not but that you will or I will the other left still
   stunned by love

we talk of rituals how clothes are burned or stones gathered
   acts to release the dead
I leave a bowl of candies for grandfather's sweet tooth you sing
   a long lost child asleep for its mother
so many ways of passing through grief reaching into another
   land with gestures of gratitude
knowing they were ours and are and that we breathe each
   death as our own

stronger than a dust devil the sand spout whacks my back your
   head buried in my chest
something is there and we know it standing in the ocean's
   wreckage of shells and feathers
your dog leaping joyfully around us I know what has passed
   through is good
I'm in your terrain you know the spirits here I remember
   grandfather's farm

a horse stands in the sleet there is no shelter and maybe there is
   no horse
it's almost impossible to stand so still that your shadow creeps
   into your shape
wind rakes the grass a gull with a hook in its mouth flounders
   like an old shirt in the sky
there's nowhere to go we turn toward each other and call our
   names on the beach

annual physical

standing there with an overflowing urine sample in hand
  muscle control not quite what it was or the will
cotton batten and tape on the inner elbow cholestoral globs
  thickening my blood in the lab
my knee aches where I wrenched it on a slippery step nine
  months ago my ears ringing I can't be deaf
wondering what I know for sure I keep doing that at these
  moments though there's no real question

and it doesn't matter anymore it's just an impulse an old bluff
  a way of finding out
as if I'm not interested in cause and effect as if I'm not
  interested in cures and I'm not
just staring at the bottle my fingers wet with piss thinking I
  might have to shake someone's hand
thinking too that my car might not start thinking of roses
  the beautiful cliche they are

there's no cure when there's no disease and there's no disease
  unless we say so
how we look at things or hear them a fir tree in the wind
  a man's last breath flowing out
how we want to live in another body layers of sweaters and
  coats the deepest ideology
I've been to the sick room everyone dying of cures I've seen
  the madness of healers

I've lain in bed after love the late afternoon drifting in through
  the window
I've watched my lover dressing her slender body for dinner and
  I'm hungry once again
how could I wish anything other than what is this work this
  preparing of tables?

the miracle is here with its odours there are flies in the house and
light on the sill

the angels I know sweat and live by rivers they are intimidated
by God
I keep calling out like a sacrifice laid on the altar of someone
else's belief
the lost and found is filled with ideas don't think about that
too much
there's nothing to heal I speak with one tongue and two voices
at least

nothing's new the heart of earth in flames and someone
drumming at the door
this is the heat we live through spinning and pelting our way
through dark skies
I'm telling you I don't have time for the bluff I want everything
straight
the laboratory is humming someone wants to get in and I'm
getting out

wanting

wanting everything wanting nothing
each night rain comes down
slopping over the eaves
each night I lie there loving
the water the 4 a.m. birds
outside my window
loud and urgent
and I thank them
pray for their ancient bones
and their impersonal eyes

nothing changes
bird has been bird
slipping into our history
nothing changes
the beautiful song
as I lie there
anxious with betrayal
wanting a lot less but clear
nothing changes
but the angle of my head my eyes
how my ear hears
a trifle differently
the same words
and so wants more or less

wanting

fewer questions

I ask fewer questions

I'm not old not young

my body still pulses
from making love this afternoon

I wonder at her beauty
the sun's heat beside the pond

I am getting used to my body
what it allows
I'm getting used to pain
what it is

somewhere the ground opens for me
among the trees where I lived
or the garden with its earth and tendrils

five decades are gone
they were never really here
though sometimes I find traces in my body

like the decades
I disappear
I don't know where
I'd like to say here or there
put words to it

I read less
as if I am becoming illiterate
or there is nothing to know

because there are swallows beneath the eaves
or a white dress on the line

I ask fewer questions

gift

like a saint you wait
with nothing to offer
your hands hang from your sleeves
you're barefoot in the air

I've seen you often
standing at an intersection
waiting for the light to change
I've felt your breath behind me

there is a longing
in your eyes
my pockets are empty
what is it you want?

I've been learning
not to ask for anything
I've been learning
to give it all away

and here you are
wanting something more
begging for the heart
I no longer have

I'll find you something
you've been waiting so long
I've heard you at my window
heard you in my song

you can have my birth
you already own my death
like a trumpet's silver note
everything between is gone

witness

the mourners have left
all of them carrying their various weights
shuffling slowly
the dust uneasy at their feet
they'll learn to stride again

I'm the eye
there has to be a witness
there's a sky
I'm here to negotiate

the griefstricken fade
turning to stare at the stones
they lose themselves in pity
and nostalgia's softness
the children play dead
play doctors and criminals
like all young they learn to live
rehearsing the future

I'm the eye
there has to be a witness
there's a sky
I'm here to negotiate

the dead just lie there
waiting for parole
perhaps there's freedom in this
all the laws are broken
and there's nothing to obey

I'm the eye
there has to be a witness
there's a sky
I'm here to negotiate

arriving

wondering how we lose light our eyes narrowing to blindness
remembering when I looked the sun in the eye unflinchingly
strategies of fear how we make the world small enough to explain

listening to someone preach the great divide what's known and not
riding old jack across the sky dragging the sun behind us
homilies of pride breaking the world into pieces that fit

hugging the child with ropes a terrible human love
lurching through the barroom door into the arms of the lord
alibis of failure how we keep saving the world until it dies

hanging around nightclubs or church looking for the messiah
praying for a bullet or rain anything to slow the pain
rituals of worship how we try to put the world to sleep

clinging in the end to life as if it's someone's pantleg
grasping for words something to shape the air
sacraments of smoke and surrender to the earth

gasping at the beauty of the sudden fall
arriving then arriving arriving

{Here's something rare. No dates and a strange name. She used to walk the country roads all dressed up. A nice dress with flowers, a hat with a veil, white shoes and a white purse. Sundays. Never saw her during the week. Don't know anyone that knew who she was. Just walking along the dirt roads outside of town. Carried herself well, you know, straight-backed, head up, looking kind of proud. Real skinny. People called her Crazy Bone. Or, just plain Crazy. I offered her a ride once. She kept walking. Gave me a smile though. Can't say I ever heard of anyone she talked to. She was just there. You got used to her. Don't quite know when she disappeared. People began to wonder about her, asking each other if they'd seen Crazy last Sunday. Police got involved, asking around, checking out the country roads, but there wasn't a trace, and no one knew where she came from anyway. Or, where she went. Eventually a few people got together, went to the town council and suggested a plot be donated for Crazy. There was some talk. Some people thought it was not a good idea at all, what if she was still alive. Most felt she deserved a resting place, even if we didn't know where she ended up. Strange, isn't it? A lifetime of Sunday's, and she's gone. Like I said, all dressed up.

Oh, this one, this is the woman saw most of us into the world. She had healing hands they said, could run her fingers down your backbone and find just where it was out of place and she'd click it back in a second. You'd hardly notice her doing it, but you sure felt better.

Delivered my oldest, can't complain. After that we had a doctor in town, and everyone went to him. Fine old gent, made the rounds in those days, knew your family inside out. If you were out of work, he wouldn't charge you, or maybe you'd go over and paint the trim on his house.

But this one, she had a bit of the other world in her. Knew what you were thinking before you thought it. Healing hands and wide-awake eyes. Could find water, too, with a stick.

You know, when she passed on, there was no one to take her place. We had the doc, and the rest, well, just didn't seem any need for it. The well-driller found our water. The older I get, though, I find myself wondering about her, her hands, her eyes.

Over here, this is where my wife's laid.

A good woman, a happy soul. It was her gift. Happiness. And it spread to all those around her. Made me a different man, for sure.

Where She Is, Is Joy.

And where she's been.

Beside her, that's where my stone goes up.

Before she died, she told me to get married again, to be happy, but how could I? I didn't have the heart left.

Yes, they'll plant me here, beside my wife, and that'll be the end of that story.

But, the stonelicker, I don't know. Could be he got resurrected.}

plum tree

beneath a plum tree
in blossom
a rat scuttling
for home
a crow staring
from a roof
not everything
ends here
though I've forgotten
to keep time
and I paid
the man
with the spade

come with me

come with me
breath for breath
my companion
breathing in
breathing out
come with me
till that breath
going out
going out
and you pause
for a moment
between breaths
and that's so long
so long
and I'll go on
while you return
to the room
and the sun
on the sill

see me out
with your dark eyes
and your hand
on me

in memorium

they've come to dance
not at midnight but at noon
thin men in their flapping suits
women in dark swirling skirts

breathlessly
silently
the hungry ghosts
pirouette
a wild dance
of desire

ragtime or waltz
andante and adagio
simple time
in memorium

no one sees them
the town so busy
with its life
trying to make ends meet
no one sees them
the sun hot at noon
and the radio
playing news

for a moment they dance
in their loose clothes
till they're out of time
and return

here for its skin

some days I'm sinking
into this silent town
familiar fingers
around my ankles

are these hands
repellent or welcome?
I lose the question
like a dream

someone is shaving
with a straight razor
a cat sharpens
its claws on the couch

already I don't belong
to the clarity of things
everything slips away
behind its shade

there's just this love
muddy and uncombed
there's this love
that goes unredeemed

and I'm here for its skin
for its breath and cry
learning the ecstasy
of its solitude

I will cut you a diamond

I want to say something simple
I want to stroke your hair

there's so much eternity ahead of us

will we find our way?
my hands don't know you anymore
I turn them now to work

will we find our way?
there are no shoes beneath the bed
I am learning to disappear

there is so much eternity

I will cut you a diamond
crossing itself with light
take it out when you are old
and hold it to the sun

I will remember you
tell me about the world
remind me of what I miss
the way rain falls in july
the way lovers sometimes weep when they kiss

I want to sit with you
I want to stroke your hair

the door

so
the door
swings in
and you're here
I can smell you
beside the bed
hear your shoes
scuffing the tiles
there's not much to say
nothing really
and the door
swings out
so

the hand of my beloved

today it's so close
smelling like rose petals
it brushes across
the back of my hand
it's bending
toward my ear
and it doesn't matter
if I listen
because I know
what will be whispered

a moment earlier
when I thought
I had a choice
or something to say
I was in panic
how one stops breathing
before a closed door
afraid of the winter
before it arrives
and trembling with poverty

now it's here
a surveyer
on a long road
gazing at me
a rolled map
beneath his arm
wondering
how to tell me
my coordinates
are known

there's nothing to decide
it's all come to this
after all the hoopla
a quiet mathematics
what I am I am
a dignity I trust
a last look
into my children's eyes
and the hand oh god
of my beloved

empty coat

an empty coat
dangling from an elm
in march
icicles dripping
from its sleeves

footprints arriving
beneath the coat
but not leaving
a yellow scarf
sailing in the wind

tell me ma
where I've been
the streets are bare
the sky is dark
and I can't find my skin

dream

nothing
but a willow tree
an umbrella
and the rain
drizzling
down

a long footprint

this place
I live
between exhaustion
and the word
wired
by unknown sources
currents flowing
just beneath the skin

the unrelieved
blue sky
the wind

all I am

I longed to leave the electric storm of my town but found when
 I left the storm was in me

I am not forgiven my sins they remain teaching me slowly to
 live with them

the call
from the dead
in my flesh

alive alive alive

nothing is erased
only forgotten
for a while

a moment a day
a thousand years

at this moment
because of an island
of cloud
passing by
I remember
a long footprint
on a beach
at lake winnipeg

because of a footprint
other places
other things
father in pajamas
winding his watch
a shadow in his lung
a curtain billowing out
and great-grandmother
calling out gently
at death

realizing
what a blessed day
this has been
my body awake
windows wide open
to the world
and the cat
asleep in the bathtub
downstairs

yearning toward what is alive or was memory's rapacity
  for earth's details the exact moment

desire's circle all self wanting to live and live again the
  daughter mothering her mother

grandfather
young and shoeless
in a photograph
the bleached skulls
of horses
water rippling
across my feet
this place
between moments
everything always
about to shift

words
for lost things
a face a name
how a hand moved
to cover a smile

weather
on the street
inside the heart

all I am

I didn't know what it was shadowed me all these years
  turns out it's me

looking over my shoulder at what I've been nothing random
  anymore but a figure fully shaped

on my heels
and picking up
after me

all I am

the animal sitting on the sill

a yellow dress

a yellow dress
hanging on the line
children sleeping
in the shade

guitar's unstrung
horn filled with dirt
the sexton's boots
are caked with clay

someone's jazz
from a window sill
radio's dead
the blues played out

when the saints go marching in

grandmother knitting
on her bench
yarn unravelling
in the grass

shovel leaning
against a stone
vines tangled
along the arch

the stranger
is leaving town
the sun slanting
off his chrome

when the saints go marching in

barn's dark door

grain flies
in a perfect arc
from her hand
she is surrounded
by brown hens
and a red rooster

the sun is high
she wipes her brow
with the back
of one hand
wisps of white hair
at her temples

she looks at me
her eyes wrinkling
as she smiles
turning
and enters
the barn's dark door

caught in the sky

your bones she said
are the bones
of everyone before you
only the night
when you look in the mirror
is yours

this business called god
gets out of hand
it's practically inhuman
what you see
looking back at you
turns you away

it's what you are
that ancient bird
caught in the sky
landing sometimes
here
among the dead

remember the dead
speak of them
and death's charisma
they are nothing
but memory
and memory is short

remember me she says
her dress hanging
on a hook
the enamel basin
filled with rain
and clouds

gravedigger

his foot on the spade
the gravedigger looks at his watch
once again time begins
with this betrayal

earth gives to the spade
he can feel it along his leg
his shoulders bunching
to toss the dirt aside

he sweats in the sun
thinking for a moment
of his wife in the garden
her grey hair pulled back

a carpenter rides a roof
to the ringing of his hammer
and the song about
a red hen and a rooster

tectonic plates shift
beneath the pacific
in town the stone cutter
doesn't know

home st.

a guest
on this dangerous street
in this town
a guest
who has lost his eyes
feeling his way
through the light

sockets
turned to the sky
too often born
a ghost in awe
and worn
an old coat
on sticks

blind as light
and unseen
a shade
beneath the maple
waiting
to see
the lovely one

a guest
without
an invitation
with one foot
on the wheel
and nothing left
to hold

joker

who else
in the end
to sing to
but god here
a joker
the god of graves

who I talk to
wandering
among the stones
and the smile
that sorrow
becomes

there must be
an end to grief
so that things
may change
the hand turning
to work

change change change

the windows are all broken
and wind blows through the house
we are reading holy scriptures
waiting for our guests
but we don't know who they are

the dead return in their formal clothes
barefoot and wandering through open doors
they bang into things to let us know
and when we turn to wonder
they whisper *change change change*

and we nod and remember
and return to our books
the dead weeping softly
reach to embrace their lovers
pale kisses on their lips

giacometti's loneliness remains
the sculptor's hands become stone
we step carefully around graves
to avoid grasping hands
the dead are so evangelical

old tom

the deaf cat howls
at first light
a kind of statement
I guess
about creation
coming alive each day
the surprise of it
how long the night
must seem
its anticipation
fear moving to wonder
and yet the assertion
in that howl
a gratitude turning
to irritation
old tom pissed off
at the day
he yearns for
each night
unfree in his need
caught deaf
and thankful
for light
staggering
through the silence
nothing of him
in the world
but a howl

dead's dead

rain coming down hard
that's all
no sorrow no joy
no nothing
rain pitting the dirt
in the flower bed

yes I remember
a rain like this
drubbing the roof
in st. james
me half-asleep
after a night's work

or pelting
the kitchen window
on woodlawn crescent
white sox and dodgers
on the radio

or another time
say on kitchener
or grant

rain
all day all week
on east 3rd
vancouver winter
dreamed up
by bergman

the dead
everywhere
are dead
in my apartment
on the balcony
my mouth
open to the rain
I'm alive
for now
remembering
things

no one
at the window
no one
on the phone

god loves everyone
the sparrow on the ground

dead's dead

sexton

the old man
head bowed
to his work
snips a dead blade
from the tall gladiolus
yellow mouths
drinking the sky

this time around

let this fall like cold clear water to your ear
a breeze in summer and plums splitting in a bowl
the shade of a man standing in the garden
calling to the crows a song from a vanished soul

yardwork

spear grass
a scythe

yes

Patrick Friesen is the author of *Blasphemer's Wheel*, winner of the Manitoba Book of the Year Award and runner-up for the Milton Acorn People's Poetry Award. *A Broken Bowl* was short-listed for the Governor General's Award. His most recent work *St. Mary at Main* was shortlisted for the Dorothy Livesay Poetry Prize. He has also written for stage, radio, TV and film. He lives in Vancouver where he teaches writing at Kwantlen University College.